A Note to Parents

DK READERS is a compelling programme for beginning
readers, designed in conjunction with leading literacy
experts, including Maureen Fernandes, B.Ed (Hons).
Maureen has spent many years teaching literacy, both
in the classroom and as a specialist in schools.

Beautiful illustrations and superb full-colour photographs
combine with engaging, easy-to-read stories to offer a fresh
approach to each subject in the series. Each DK READER is
guaranteed to capture a child's interest while developing his
or her reading skills, general knowledge and love of reading.

The five levels of DK READERS are aimed at different
reading abilities, enabling you to choose the books that
are exactly right for your child:

Pre-level 1: Learning to read
Level 1: Beginning to read
Level 2: Beginning to read alone
Level 3: Reading alone
Level 4: Proficient readers

The "normal" age at which a child begins
to read can be anywhere from three to
eight years old. Adult participation
through the lower levels is very
helpful for providing encouragement,
discussing storylines and sounding
out unfamiliar words.

No matter which level you select,
you can be sure that you are
helping your child '
read, then read to

D1512357

DK | Penguin Random House

For Dorling Kindersley
Editor Shari Last
Senior Designer David McDonald
Slipcase Designer Stefan Georgiou
Pre-Production Producer Kavita Varma
Senior Producer Alex Bell
Managing Editor Sadie Smith
Managing Art Editor Ron Stobbart
Creative Manager Sarah Harland
Art Director Lisa Lanzarini
Publisher Julie Ferris
Publishing Director Simon Beecroft

Reading Consultant Maureen Fernandes

DK India
Editor Rahul Ganguly
Senior Editor Garima Sharma
Assistant Art Editor Suzena Sengupta
Deputy Managing Art Editor Neha Ahuja
Pre-Production Manager Sunil Sharma

For Lucasfilm
Executive Editor J. W. Rinzler
Art Director Troy Alders
Keeper of the Holocron Leland Chee
Director of Publishing Carol Roeder

This edition published in 2016
First published in Great Britain in 2014
by Dorling Kindersley Limited,
80 Strand, London, WC2R 0RL

Slipcase UI: 001-305129-Oct/16

A CIP catalogue record for this book
is available from the British Library

ISBN: 978-1-4093-5251-8

Printed in China.

www.starwars.com
www.dk.com

A WORLD OF IDEAS:
SEE ALL THERE IS TO KNOW

Contents

DK READERS

BEGINNING
2
TO READ ALONE

STAR WARS™

THE
ADVENTURES
OF C-3PO

Written by Shari Last

Hello!

I am C-3PO.

How may I help you?

What's that?

You don't want my help?

You want to hear
about my adventures?
Well, that is a strange request.

But, of course, I am
programmed to be of service.
Now, where shall I begin?

Master Ani

I was built on the
planet Tatooine by
a young slave boy
named Anakin
Skywalker.

I called him "Master Ani".
He wanted to build a droid
helper for his mother.

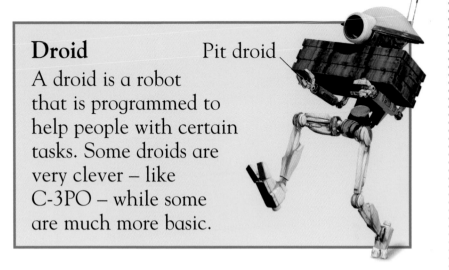

Droid   Pit droid

A droid is a robot
that is programmed to
help people with certain
tasks. Some droids are
very clever – like
C-3PO – while some
are much more basic.

Of course, I am much
cleverer than a regular droid.
I can speak more than
six million languages.

But I still helped Master Ani
and his mother because I was
a service droid and I always
obeyed my master.

A Quiet Life

I like it when
things are
peaceful and quiet.

It gives me time
to recharge my
computer brain.

I am programmed to help
people communicate.
I am not built for battle.

But everything changed when
Master Ani grew older and
became a Jedi Knight. I travelled
with him to faraway planets and
joined him on many adventures!

Droid Mix-up

Once, Master Anakin and I went to the planet Geonosis where we discovered a secret droid factory.

C-3PO's head on a battle droid!

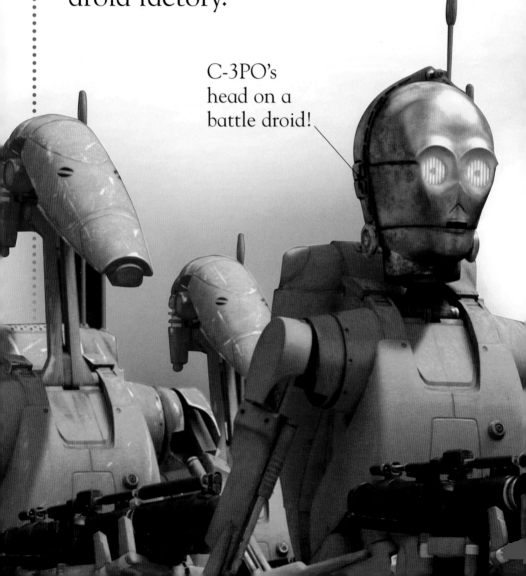

Droid factory
There are many droid factories on Geonosis. In them, huge machines build thousands of battle droids.

Unfortunately, I fell into the factory and became all mixed up with a dangerous battle droid.

I was so distressed when I found myself right in the middle of a scary battle.

Cheeky Best Friend

R2-D2 is a cheeky little astromech droid.

We met on Tatooine and have been best friends ever since.

R2-D2 is very brave and clever, but he often likes to be rude and silly!

Astromech droids
Astromech droids, such as R2-D2, are small and clever droids. They fix broken starships and help with navigation.

Don't worry. I always tell
him what to do.

And he listens to
me… sometimes.

Oh No… Jawas!

One of the things I hate
most is getting lost.
I like to feel safe.

So you can
imagine how
upset I was when
R2-D2 and I
were captured
by a group of
horrible Jawas.

Jawas live in the deserts of
Tatooine and sell scrap metal.

First of all, I am not scrap metal.
Secondly, their massive
sandcrawler vehicle
was very dirty!

Jawas
Jawas are small, scary
creatures with glowing
yellow eyes. They will sell
anything they find, so
don't get too close!

A Friendly Droid

I have made lots of new
friends on my adventures.

Jedi Knight Luke Skywalker
bought me from the Jawas.
He is my new master now,
but he is also my friend.

Princess Leia

Chewbacca

Luke's sister is Princess Leia.
She goes on secret missions to
make the galaxy a safer place.

Han Solo is a pilot.
His best friend, Chewbacca,
is a tall, hairy Wookiee.

Luke Skywalker

Han Solo

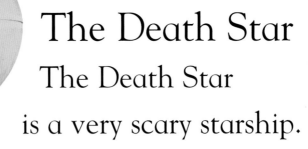

The Death Star

The Death Star

is a very scary starship.

But Master Luke is not

afraid of anything. We went

to the Death Star to rescue a

prisoner, Princess Leia.

But my friends Leia, Han

and Luke got trapped in a

rubbish masher, which was

about to squash them!

I am proud to tell you
that I saved them.
I told R2-D2 to turn off the
rubbish masher just in time.
What a close call!

Blown to Bits

One of my worst adventures
was on Cloud City.
I walked into the wrong room –
and was blown to bits!
It was very upsetting.

Luckily, my friend Chewbacca
picked up all my pieces.
He carried me around
in a rucksack until he
had time to mend me.
Even though he made a few
mistakes when putting me back
together, I was very grateful.

Working for Jabba

Jabba the Hutt is a big, slimy, disgusting creature!
He loves capturing and bothering innocent people.

He captured me once and
forced me to be his translator.
I hated it!

When I worked for Jabba,
I was treated with no respect –
even by his pet, Salacious Crumb!

I was very pleased when
Master Luke defeated Jabba
and rescued me.

Salacious Crumb
This is Jabba's
favourite pet. He must
make Jabba laugh at
least once a day or he
will be in big trouble.

Ewok Admirers

I often think that none of my friends truly appreciate how wonderful and special I am. The Ewoks do, though.

Ewoks are small, tough creatures who live on the forest moon of Endor.

The Ewoks were fascinated by my shiny gold body. They listened to everything I said, and they helped my friends and me on our mission.

To the Rescue!

Once, R2-D2 and I were
hiding in the forest of Endor
when a group of stormtroopers
captured our friends.

I wanted to help my friends,
so I shouted to the stormtroopers
and they came chasing after me.

But I tricked them!
When they came
near, an army of
Ewoks jumped out
of the trees and
helped us defeat
the stormtroopers.
Hooray!

Stormtroopers
Stormtroopers are soldiers
who work for an evil Empire.
They wear white armour
and carry deadly blasters.

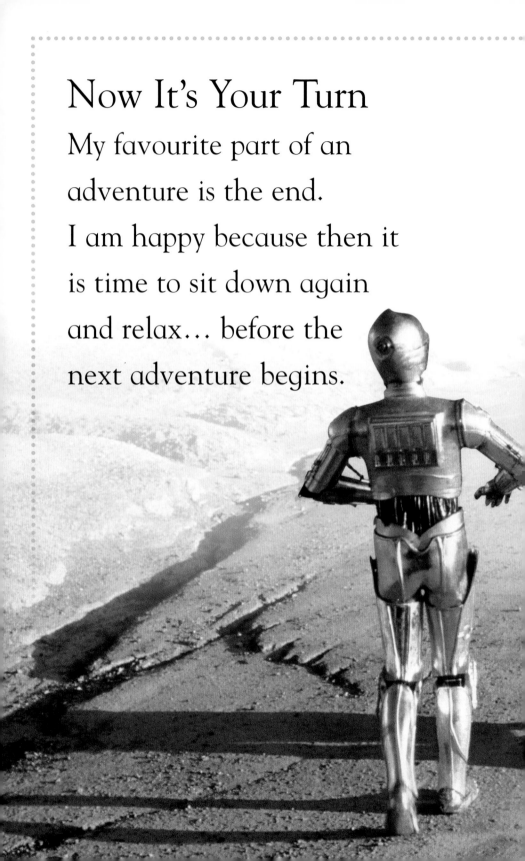

Now It's Your Turn

My favourite part of an
adventure is the end.
I am happy because then it
is time to sit down again
and relax… before the
next adventure begins.

But remember, you don't have to fly in starships or travel around the galaxy to have amazing adventures.

You can go on an exciting adventure wherever you are!

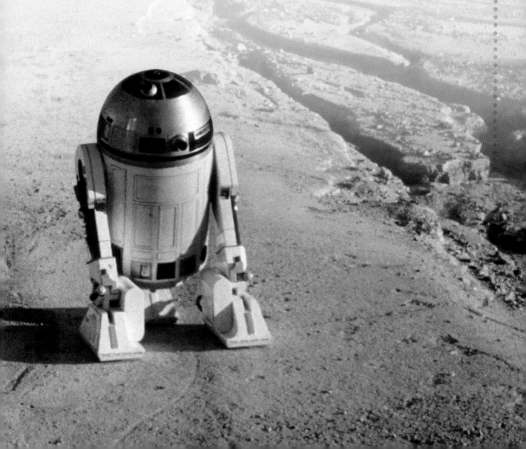

Quiz

1. On which planet are the droid factories?

2. Who is C-3PO's best friend?

3. What creatures sell scrap metal on Tatooine?

4. Where was Princess Leia held prisoner?

5. Who is Jabba the Hutt's pet?

Answers:
1. Geonosis
2. R2-D2
3. Jawas
4. On the Death Star
5. Salacious Crumb

Index